Frog Sat

by Lynn Maslen Kertell
pictures by Sue Hendra

Scholastic Inc.
New York • Toronto • London • Auckland • Sydney • Mexico City • New Delhi • Hong Kong

Ask for Bob Books at your local bookstore, or visit www.bobbooks.com.

ISBN 978-0-545-34824-9

12 11 10 9 8 7 6 5 4 3 2 1   11 12 13 14 15/0

Printed in China / 68
This edition printing, January 2011

A frog sat on a bed.

Get off the bed, frog. Go in the pond.

A cub sat on a rug.

Get off the rug, cub. Go to the den.

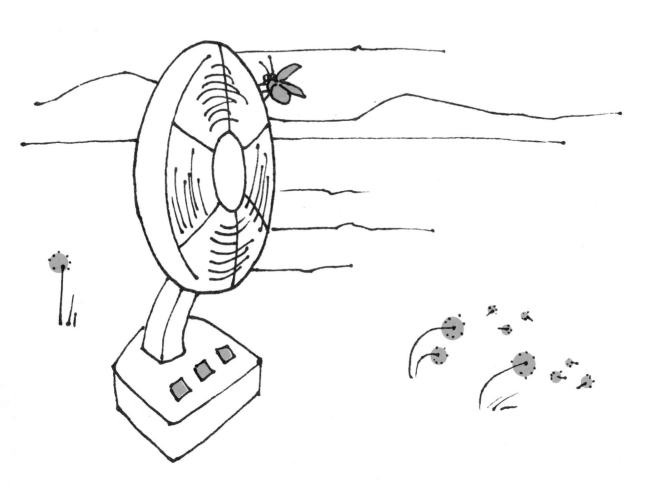

A bug sat on a fan.

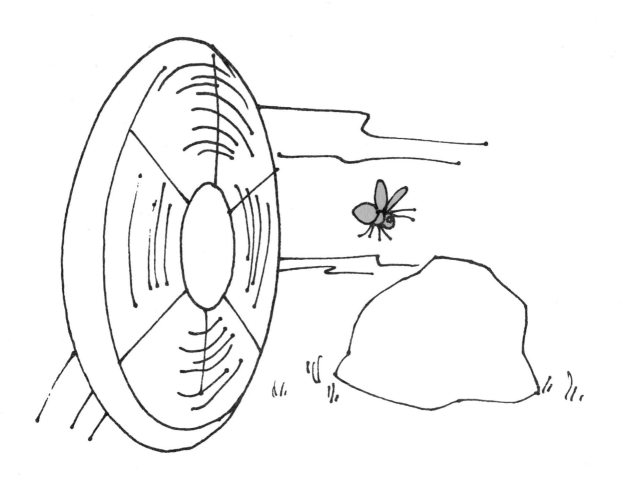

Get off the fan, bug. Go on a rock.

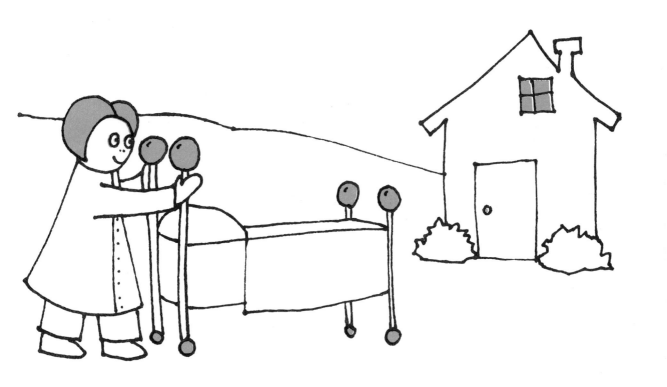

Go get the bed, Ted.

Go get the rug and fan.

Ted has the bed, rug, and fan.
O.K. Ted.

The End